THE MID NIGHT THOUGHTS

RUDRAKSH MISHRA

Copyright © Rudraksh Mishra
All Rights Reserved.

This book has been published with all efforts taken to make the material error-free after the consent of the author. However, the author and the publisher do not assume and hereby disclaim any liability to any party for any loss, damage, or disruption caused by errors or omissions, whether such errors or omissions result from negligence, accident, or any other cause.

While every effort has been made to avoid any mistake or omission, this publication is being sold on the condition and understanding that neither the author nor the publishers or printers would be liable in any manner to any person by reason of any mistake or omission in this publication or for any action taken or omitted to be taken or advice rendered or accepted on the basis of this work. For any defect in printing or binding the publishers will be liable only to replace the defective copy by another copy of this work then available.

Contents

Contents

Preface

FELICITY IN A MYSTERIOUS LAND ~Rudraksh Mishra
A FEARFUL NIGHT ~Sarthak Singh
TACTLESS SPIRIT ~Rudraksh Mishra

vi

Acknowledgements

ABOUT THE AUTHORS

Rudraksh Mishra:

Rudraksh Mishra was born on 6th December 2007 in Lucknow. His habit of being eager to know why and how of everything, exploring the concept of things made him unique in the crowd. He showed up interest in writing from the age of 5-6. The essays or stories he used to write were not of the level of an average 5-6 year old kid. Started his writing career with short stories and essays, sent to local newspapers got published, received a little fame in local presses. He never suppressed himself, he kept pushing himself and at the age of 13 he published his first book, not a good one but it was a short article about parallel worlds.

A young author Writing from a very young age, mainly a fiction writer, writes poems relating to modern day Society. Got featured in columns of various newspapers. An internationally published author. Author of The lost friend and The secret existence (only the preview is released till date) featured in magazines like sun magazine poetry foundation and many more. Currently ruling the Asia top charts 2022.

Rudraksh Mishra

Sarthak Singh:

Sarthak Singh, He Was Born On 28th July 2007 In Gonda. He was Fond Of Writing From A Very Young age. He Mainly Write Poems. And Short Stories. He Shared His Poem With Some Of His Friend. And Recently He Got An Offer To Collaborate For This Book.

Sarthak Singh

CHAPTER ONE

SPECIAL GRIND

They Wanna Change My Thought....
I Think I Have Been Caught....
In Their Mind Trap....
As If I Am A Handicap....
   With Me They Wanna Stay....
But There's No Chance Of Replay....
There's No Hurry It's Already Delay....
Are You Searching Of Me, I Am Already Away....
   I Think About It Everyday....
I Am Still Afraid Of Walking On The Way....
Whatever I Got Yesterday....
I Don't Wanna Get It Today....
   They Wanna Change My Mind....
With Them, They Wanna Me To Bind....
If They Are Able They Can Find....
I Am All Here For The Grind....

CHAPTER TWO

THE LAST SCREAM

Sometimes i really want to cry
I really don't know why
i wish i could scream and shout
speak my heart out and loud
    Trapped inside bones
wrapped with skin
whatever i am, i am alone
whatever they do, i gonna win
    Days passed in silence
mind full of violence
the unkindness kindness they give
the respectful rudeness they will receive
    My heart has turned too numb
oh! am way too dumb
All the way i came
now, just waiting for the end
    My heart is way too heavy now
Too hard to carry tell me how?
with no more paths to follow
my heart is hollow

The ocean of emptiness
The ocean of nothingness
living in a world of hatefulness
everyone gone wow! still am good how?
    I really don't know,
really don't know

CHAPTER THREE

MODERN AGE PRIMITIVES

Crushed by society
Flushed his ideas
The winged child will be
brushed by a butchering world
MODERN AGE PRIMITIVES!
　　Brushing teeth is considered important
Brushing deeds is not known
The mind full of thoughts
vs
The mindless copycats
MODERN AGE PRIMITIVES
　　The innovation burned alive
The mouth was shut by laces
That was the end of already dead hopes
MODERN AGE PRIMITIVES
　　The magical world that we live in,
Faces inside faces
Acid in mind
Still alive,isn't these the magical powers
MODERN AGE PRIMITIVES

The brilliant minded world
Finishing streotyping by streotyping
Supporting dictorship for democracy
MODERN AGE PRIMITIVES
MODERN AGE PRIMITIVES!!
THE BEGINNING OF AN END

CHAPTER FOUR

THIEVES

Thieves jumped in his home
He was all all alone
Doors none closed
His life a cyclone
    Thieves asked for money
He was like a real bunny
Nah! it isn't funny
He was like a real bunny
    Thieves searching for their happiness
Their searching ends with emptiness
His life filled with loneliness
How can he have happiness
    Thieves were curious
Oh! They found something precious
A key to something precious
They did not got anything precious....
    Thieves asked him the reason
His life made full of collisions
His life with no ambition
That's why he ain't precious
    Thieves left his home
He was all all alone

His life a cyclone
He was really all alone
    Doors alone closed,
But no one to come close
His life full of heavy blows
Now, all doors are closed
    Coz he was!!!

CHAPTER FIVE

HEALTHY MIND

My brain is like a river stream
it flows out when there is to much of rain
i am confident that i can achieve my dream
it hard like breaking a chain
    i am moving forward with an improvement
they wanna help but sorry no requirement
i am gonna achieve my goal , i am confident
and for me that's sufficient
    I am not tensed about my future
i wanna spread in world like light
but the fear i have is pressure
learned from them how to fight

CHAPTER SIX

FADING MEMORIES

I am ignored for...

The dream I have never seen
the words I said but I really didn't mean
The person I would have never been
I had not hurt someone
But still they say my heart isn't clean
    I really don't care hat you thing about
I will only do what my educator taught
I am getting for what I never did
the thing which I never thought
    i swear i gave my best
but believe me i got the worst
i tried to escape but they lure me
if there is then plz cure me
    i am ignored for...

CHAPTER SEVEN

AMUSING GROCERY

One day at a grocery shop,
I met a man selling shirts,
For money he wanted to swap,
But I really wanted some hurts.

   "Got any hurts?" I asked.
"For that's how I'll spend my money."
"No hurts here!" said the guy.
He seemed to find it quite funny.

   "We've got some lovely cakes,
I'll give you a very fine price."
"I'd rather have some sweepstakes."
The man blinked rapidly thrice.

   The man seemed exceptionally small,
And his manner was strangely amused.
He wasn't what I would call all,
Great disdain he noticeably oozed.

   Like others, he thought I was odd,
Some say I'm a bit tall.
Still he gave me a courteous nod,
As if he thought I was plenty cool.

So in search of my goal I departed,
But before the grocery shop could I leave,
The man came running full-hearted,
"I can help you I believe."
    "Shirts, hurts, you shall find.
Cakes, sweepstakes, you can get.
You must now open your mind,
And get down to Orange Street Market.

CHAPTER EIGHT

LET THE HEART SPEAK

Finding fault with everyone
not today,not tomorrow but always
    Spreading criticism for everyone
Crushing thoughts of everyone
not today, not tomorrow but always
    Thinking ignoring is a class
Drinking ego a full of glass
not today, not tomorrow but always
    Praying for the best
Procastinating all the very rest
not today, not tomorrow but always
    Breaking the windows of hope
Cracking the glorious wall of hope
not today, not tomorrow but always
    Living in their own virtual world
Still giving lectures on rituals
not today, not tomorrow but always
    Not today, not tomorrow but always
The never ending philosphical war between
Profound Socialists

Vs
The open-minded captalists

CHAPTER NINE

HAVE FAITH IT WILL BE GREAT

Have faith , it will be great
hate does not bring you fame
blaming doest not make you great
claiming doest not make it yours
have faith , it will be great
    Go through hell but do it well
fall but rise high in the sky
cry but move in a thrusty way
have faith , it will be great
    Wait the best date will come
be a dumb in public
so you wont bear jealousy
wait , you will make a legacy
    Have faith, it will be great

CHAPTER TEN

GRACE

Her smile as like grace
Though it cannot be replaced.
Her laugh so loud
It echoed through the crowd
    Her perfume scent so sweet
without it I feel incomplete
Her presence was warm
Now gone, We are left to mourn.
    It was a Friday
she sat on her driveway
Tears ran down her cheeks
Writing a letter she let her speak
    Feeling all alone
She felt her world was a cyclone
A beautiful soul
Her heart with a hole.
    She hid her depression
with no expression
She hid her sadness
    From all this madness.
    She was hurting
Considered herself as a burden

Soon things got bad
Her heart was sad

CHAPTER ELEVEN

BURIED WORDS

The words buried deep down
swallowing all pain with a beautiful smile
A beautiful fake smile for a
beautiful fake world
    Mouth shut down, wings cut down
All I as, all I was down
Killing myself yet I am alive
The prize what I got, my feelings burnt alive
    Am on a secret mission
My heart on emission
fighting with depression with no expression
Having far vision
Where I am full of ambition
    Got snakes in locality
Who bite with their power of vocality
Free falling with velocity, no connection with this drama-
city.
    Was going through hell, still doing well
Needed was perfect
Your bro was imperfect
The misery childhood I had
The misery neighbourhood I had

The better I tried
The better I failed.

IRONICAL BIRD

Whose bird is that? I think I know.
Its owner is quite happy though.
Full of joy like a vivid rainbow,
I watch him laugh. I cry hello.

　He gives his bird a shake,
And laughs until her belly aches.
The only other sound's the break,
Of distant waves and birds awake.

　The bird is huge, content and deep,
But he has promises to keep,
After cake and lots of sleep.
Sweet dreams come to him cheap.

　He rises from his gentle bed,
With thoughts of kittens in his head,
He eats his jam with lots of bread.
Ready for the day ahead

CHAPTER THIRTEEN

CHARMING BLOSSOM

Roses are red,
Violets are blue,
Illustrations are amusing,
And so are you.
Orchids are white,
Ghost ones are rare,
A box is black,
And so is your hair.
Magnolia grows,
With buds like eggs,
Your form is slender,
And so are your legs.
Sunflowers reach,
Up to the skies,
My tree is hazel,
And so are your eyes.
Foxgloves in hedges,
Surround the farms,
Branches are slender,
And so are your arms.

Daisies are pretty,
Daffies have style,
A bath is warm,
And so is your smile.
A moonlight is beautiful,
Just like you.

CHAPTER FOURTEEN

THE WORLD OF ALIENS

The way in which i want to do something
the way i actually did something.
the world of the aliens
the world of their choice.
    The path i wanted to choose
the path i took .
the world of the aliens
the world of their choice.
    The life i wanted
The life i got
the castle i wanted
the warehouse i got
the world of the aliens
the world of their choice
    The cake i wanted
the fake messages i got
the world of the aliens
the world of their choice
    The true i was
that lies i got

the world of the aliens
the world of their choice
    Their sake was what i did
their jealousy was what i got
the world of the aliens
the world of their choice
    The unconditional love i gave
the heap of comparisons i got
the world of the aliens
the world of their choice
    The heat i faced , without any greed
all was that what is called a good deed
The open I was with you,
That much you betrayed
That is how evils are made.
    the world of the aliens
the world of their choice......

CHAPTER FIFTEEN

FAKE CARE

The ignorance i got
for the importance i gave
The incognisance i got
for the recognization i gave
    Trust me, they affirmed
fooled me, they confirmed
You are special they told
i too have heart they forgot
    Thought they are for life-time
forgot i am an entertainment
that too for short-time
never thought i am just their enjoyment
    Never cared the way i did
yet telling that's not fair
Tried my best to make them laugh and smile
Never asked is this my real laugh and smile
    My life is a lie
everyone saying the last bye
Them not caring for my feelings is worst,
realising it late is really worst.
    Always been a bunny
thought i am too funny

secrets they found funny
regret, it isn't funny
    I think it's the time to end the game
eyes blinking heart pumping, life too lame
Who cares ?, infact
who stays?
    My smile is good, they appreciated
faking it since childhood, now expertised
Showing as i am important
playing as i am their enjoyment

CHAPTER SIXTEEN

UNSAID REALITY

I wanna ask my soul
but it will make me befoul
I thought it would be helpful
but I never thought that it would be harmful
    They pretend to be powerful
but their intensions are still doubtful
their presence still harmful
but for many they are still faithful/ useful
    They work to complete their needs
they wanna succeed without thinking about their deeds
they only work for their greed
Transmitting their greed in their own seed
    Filled with toxicness
yet giving, lectures on kindness
then, Being rude all the day
now, becoming dude all the way
    Disgracing everyone's goal
Disgusting, minds with a hole.
Searching their door of fortune
Criticising other's goal or fortune

CHAPTER SEVENTEEN

MODERN DRAMA

Hit by a wall, got up again
Hit by reality got stuck forever
Doing well, but actually he was drowning in a well
    World so modern systems so primitive
independent countries constrained lives
Water are purified mind still runged
    Biased debates on screen are planning to stop
corruption
Faking love on social media
blood-shedding in mind
    Threw innovation in dustbin
Searching picture in the bin
Spreading Hinduism on social media
No idea about the hindu view of life
THE BEGINNING OF AN END!

CHAPTER EIGHTEEN

THE LOST HAPPINESS

I could not utter a word at that moment
It was the same which we together went
I have got my life yet
still living on rent
    I believe my dream is very auspicious
It's something to me very precious
The sake about which I was conscious
But believe me, my behaviour isn't suspicious
    I didn't have a track to run
No humour left in the jokes
that could make me laugh and have some fun
I am left all alone
now, i want to shine like a sun
    My life is like a battleground
But there is a person with whom i love to be around
After many turns in my life, i am still spellbound
I tried but i couldn't found
yes it's my happiness,
that i couldn't found

CHAPTER NINETEEN

SPECIAL PARTY

The Day Was Full Of Joy
I Was Having Every Reason To Enjoy
I Was Fear Of The Society
But It Was also for my anxiety
   It Was An Opportunity...
For Me To Express What's In My Mind...
I Gonna Say It In Front Of The Whole Community...
If And Only If She Doesn't Mind...
   I Wanna Say It With Confidence...
Ohh! It's A Dream Or A Coincidence....
But, My Tongue Slurred...
I Haven't Said What I Want To And Now I Am Incurred....
   I Think It Wasn't A Right Time....
It Was A Surprisingly State Of Yours As Well As Mine....
I Was Not Able To Deal With The Situation....
It Was Something Beyond My Imagination....
   Between Us There's A Connection....
I Know It's The Best Combination....
But Who Cares About It....
Because It's Just An Emotion....
   Ah! Bro Do You think Of Reality....
No it's Just An Illusion

CHAPTER TWENTY

I WISH I KNEW

If it was my last day
I would express my heart
Ishow the power of a bard
I wish i would be able to show how i was suppressed
to show the reasons i was depressed
    I wish i would die soon
i would say my last bye soon
wish i would never be born again
I wish i would never be a pary of this race again
    I wish i knew that, bye will be the last bye
I wish i knew that their were other actors too in the cast,
why?
    The one who saved me from depression is the same,
who paved my way to depression
The true and the true really cares, turned into
really, who stays ? who cares?
    I wish i could know if it was a coincidence,
Or it was showing sequence of consequences
The habit of talking everyday turned into,
the habit of ignoring and stalking everyday

CHAPTER TWENTY-ONE

GRACE OF MIND

The Ascent Of My Mind....
That Wants Me To Look Behind....
But There's No Feature Of Rewind....
Having Dust In My Eye, But I Am Not Blind....
    I am not blind
i can see what's happening with me
the night i slept crying
i wept my tears lying
    Is That A Mountain?
That They Wanna Climb....
Or is it a Fountain?
That They Wanna Find....
    They Wanna Make Me Cry....
Our Thoughts May Vary....
I Am Not Afraid, There's No Worry....
They Are Still Waiting For Me To Bury....
    My Mind Is Still Developing....
But It Knows Everything....
It's The State Of Beginning....
Also The State Of Wondering....

CHAPTER TWENTY-TWO

THE PEN CRIES

They talk about my soul
They think i am befoul
They wanna make me fool
But I am, calm and cool
    They don't wanna see others happy
They only make themselves happy
They live in royalty
But i know their reality
    They pretend to be royal
but they aren't so loyal
They wanna take a fight
But I wanna say, don't mess with light
    Are they child?
That they wanna play
I think they are wild
Oh! that's a forest where they stay.
    They show they love me
But I know, they hate me
They show that they are caring
But I know, they hate sharing

CHAPTER TWENTY-THREE

DIVINE LIGHT

Living my life, not sure what is right
fighting with my mind, i am not doing it right
controlling my anger
discussing with so many langers/discussing with a langer
    Empty mind, devil's house
People with no mind, devil's spouse
I was the one who was left
Without any treasures i was theft
    Living in a magical world
believing in a world of tragic heards
Stop giving me motivating words
I dont wanna live in a world of stupid heads
    They Pretend To Be Wild....
But They Behave Like A Child....
They Show Care For Me....
Are They Really Concerned For Me?
    They Wanna Achieve Their Goal....
They Have Dirty Mind As Coal....
They Pretend To Be Cool....
Or They Just Wanna Make Us Fool....

CHAPTER TWENTY-FOUR

THE GHOST AND THE LADY

See the hooting of the ghost,
I think he's angry at the beef roast.
He finds it hard to see the panda,
Overshadowed by the odd vanda.
Who is that flapping near the king?
I think she'd like to eat the growth ring.
She is but a keen lady,
Admired as she sits upon a gentlelady.
Her sharp car is just a lobster,
It needs no gas, it runs on mobster.
She's not alone she brings an ace,
a pet camel, and lots of bass
The camel likes to chase a girlfriend,
Especially one that's in the weekend.
The ghost shudders at the strange wolf
He want to leave but she wants the seawolf.

CHAPTER TWENTY-FIVE

FELICITY IN A MYSTERIOUS LAND

Once upon a time there was a delightful girl called Felicity Thomas. She was on the way to see her Michelle Thomas, when she decided to take a short cut through Snotchester Forest.

It wasn't long before Felicity got lost. She looked around, but all she could see were trees. Nervously, she felt into her bag for her favourite toy, Miss Piggy, but Miss Piggy was nowhere to be found! Felicity began to panic. She felt sure she had packed Miss Piggy. To make matters worse, she was starting to feel hungry.

Unexpectedly, she saw a wise flamingo dressed in a pink bowler hat disappearing into the trees.

"How odd!" thought Felicity.

For the want of anything better to do, she decided to follow the peculiarly dressed flamingo. Perhaps it could tell him the way out of the forest.

Eventually, Felicity reached a clearing. She found herself surrounded by houses made from different sorts of food.

There was a house made from broccoli florets, a house made from lollipops, a house made from toffees, a house made from fruit gums and a house made from macarons.

Felicity could feel her tummy rumbling. Looking at the houses did nothing to ease her hunger.

"Hello!" she called. "Is anybody there?"

Nobody replied.

Felicity looked at the roof on the closest house and wondered if it would be rude to eat somebody else's chimney. Obviously it would be impolite to eat a whole house, but perhaps it would be considered acceptable to nibble the odd fixture or lick the odd fitting, in a time of need.

A cackle broke through the air, giving Felicity a fright. A witch jumped into the space in front of the houses. She was carrying a cage. In that cage was Miss Piggy!

"Miss Piggy!" shouted Felicity. She turned to the witch. "That's my toy!"

The witch just shrugged.

"Give Miss Piggy back!" cried Felicity.

"Not on your nelly!" said the witch.

"At least let Miss Piggy out of that cage!"

Before she could reply, four wise flamingoes rushed in from a footpath on the other side of the clearing. Felicity recognised the one in the pink bowler hat that she'd seen earlier. The witch seemed to recognise him too.

"Hello Big Flamingo," said the witch.

"Good morning." The flamingo noticed Miss Piggy. "Who is this?"

"That's Miss Piggy," explained the witch.

"Ooh! Miss Piggy would look lovely in my house. Give it to me!" demanded the flamingo.

The witch shook her head. "Miss Piggy is staying with me."

"Um... Excuse me..." Felicity interrupted. "Miss Piggy lives with me! And not in a cage!"

Big Flamingo ignored her. "Is there nothing you'll trade?" he asked the witch.

The witch thought for a moment, then said, "I do like to be entertained. I'll release him to anybody who can eat a whole front door."

Big Flamingo looked at the house made from macarons and said, "No problem, I could eat an entire house made from macarons if I wanted to."

"That's nothing," said the next flamingo. "I could eat two houses."

"There's no need to show off," said the witch. Just eat one front door and I'll let you have Miss Piggy."

Felicity watched, feeling very worried. She didn't want the witch to give Miss Piggy to Big Flamingo. She didn't think Miss Piggy would like living with a wise flamingo, away from her house and all her other toys.

The other three flamingoes watched while Big Flamingo put on his bib and withdrew a knife and fork from his pocket.

"I'll eat this whole house," said Big Flamingo. "Just you watch!"

Big Flamingo pulled off a corner of the front door of the house made from lollipops. He gulped it down smiling, and went back for more.

And more.

And more.

Eventually, Big Flamingo started to get bigger - just a little bit bigger at first. But after a few more fork-fulls of lollipops, he grew to the size of a large snowball - and he was every bit as round.

"Erm... I don't feel too good," said Big Flamingo.

Suddenly, he started to roll. He'd grown so round that he could no longer balance!

"Help!" he cried, as he rolled off down a slope into the forest.

Big Flamingo never finished eating the front door made from lollipops and Miss Piggy remained trapped in the witch's cage.

Average Flamingo stepped up, and approached the house made from toffees.
"I'll eat this whole house," said Average Flamingo. "Just you watch!"

Average Flamingo pulled off a corner of the front door of the house made from toffees. She gulped it down smiling, and went back for more.

And more.

And more.

After a while, Average Flamingo started to look a little queasy. She grew greener...

...and greener.

A woodcutter walked into the clearing. "What's this bush doing here?" he asked.

"I'm not a bush, I'm a flamingo!" said Average Flamingo.

"It talks!" exclaimed the woodcutter. "Those talking bushes are the worst kind. I'd better take it away before somebody gets hurt."

"No! Wait!" cried Average Flamingo, as the woodcutter picked her up. But the woodcutter ignored her cries and carried the flamingo away under his arm.

Average Flamingo never finished eating the front door made from toffees and Miss Piggy remained trapped in the witch's cage.

Little Flamingo stepped up, and approached the house made from fruit gums.

"I'll eat this whole house," said Little Flamingo. "Just you watch!"

Little Flamingo pulled off a corner of the front door of the house made from fruit gums. He gulped it down smiling, and went back for more.

And more.

And more.

After five or six platefuls, Little Flamingo started to fidget uncomfortably on the spot.

He stopped eating fruit gums for a moment, then grabbed another forkful.

But before he could eat it, there came an almighty roar. A bottom burp louder than a rocket taking off, propelled Little Flamingo into the sky.

"Aggghhhhhh!" cried Little Flamingo. "I'm scared of heigh..."

Little Flamingo was never seen again.

Little Flamingo never finished eating the front door made from fruit gums and Miss Piggy remained trapped in the witch's cage.

Tiny Flamingo stepped up, and approached the house made from macarons.

"I'll eat this whole house," said Tiny Flamingo. "Just you watch!"

Tiny Flamingo pulled off a corner of the front door of the house made from macarons. She gulped it down smiling, and went back for more.

And more.

And more.

However, on the next mouthful, the food fell straight out of Tiny Flamingo's mouth. She tried to stuff in another forkful of macarons, but once again, the food fell out. There just wasn't enough room left in her belly.

"This is just not fair!" declared Tiny Flamingo, and stomped off into the forest.

Tiny Flamingo never finished eating the front door made from macarons and Miss Piggy remained trapped in the witch's cage.

"That's it," said the witch. "I win. I get to keep Miss Piggy."

"Not so fast," said Felicity. "There is still one front door to go. The front door of the house made from broccoli florets. And I haven't had a turn yet.

"I don't have to give you a turn!" laughed the witch. "My game. My rules."

The woodcutter's voice carried through the forest. "I think you should give her a chance. It's only fair."

"Fine," said the witch. "But you saw what happened to the flamingoes. She won't last long."

"I'll be right back," said Felicity.

"What?" said the witch. "Where's your sense of impatience? I thought you wanted Miss Piggy back."

Felicity ignored the witch and gathered a hefty pile of sticks. She came back to the clearing and started a small camp fire. Carefully, she broke off a piece of the door of the house made from broccoli florets and toasted it over the fire. Once it had cooked and cooled just a little, she took a bite. She quickly devoured the whole piece.

Felicity sat down on a nearby log.

"You fail!" cackled the witch. "You were supposed to eat the whole door."

"I haven't finished," explained Felicity. "I am just waiting for my food to go down."

When Felicity's food had digested, she broke off another piece of the door made from broccoli florets. Once more, she toasted her food over the fire and waited for it to cool just a little. She ate it at a leisurely pace then waited for it to digest.

Eventually, after several sittings, Felicity was down to the final piece of the door made from broccoli florets. Carefully, she toasted it and allowed it to cool just a little. She finished her final course. Felicity had eaten the entire front door of the house made from broccoli florets.

The witch stamped her foot angrily. "You must have tricked me!" she said. "I don't reward cheating!"

"I don't think so!" said a voice. It was the woodcutter. He walked back into the clearing, carrying his axe. "This little girl won fair and square. Now hand over Miss Piggy or I will chop your broomstick in half."

The witch looked horrified. She grabbed her broomstick and placed it behind her. Then, huffing, she opened the door of the cage.

Felicity hurried over and grabbed Miss Piggy, checking that her favourite toy was all right. Fortunately, Miss Piggy was unharmed.

Felicity thanked the woodcutter, grabbed a quick souvenir, and hurried on to meet Michelle. It was starting to get dark.

When Felicity got to Michelle's house, her threw her arms around her.

"I was so worried!" cried Michelle. "You are very late."

As Felicity described her day, she could tell that Michelle didn't believe her. So she grabbed a napkin from her pocket.

"What's that?" asked Michelle.

Felicity unwrapped a doorknob made from lollipops. "Pudding!" she said.

Michelle almost fell off her chair.

The End

42

CHAPTER TWENTY-SIX

A FEARFUL NIGHT

Once upon a time there was a boy named Sudhanshu he was having phasmophobia {phobia of ghosts}...He was living in the rural area of Indore with his friend.They both were from Bhogaon.Bhogaon a village near Agra.They were living here to earn thier living needs. Sudhanshu was doing a low level job in a big sweethouse MISHRA SWEET HOUSE. Hari {Sudhanshu's friend} was also doing a low level job in MISHRA ENTERPRISES. They were living in the houses opposite to each other's house on rent in the rural area. Their office from thier house was 15 km.

They used to wake up at 4 'o' clock and get ready to go till 6 AM.Sudhanshu was a very cheerfull and easy going guy, he always smiles and greets whenever he meet someone. Hari was a very practical guy he used to talk to himself planning the future, how to do that, what to do.

One day Hari was very tensed so as a friend Sudhanshu asked Hari that what is the problem.Hari refused to tell him at once,but Sudhanshu kept asking the same, and finally he told,and by listening to what he told Sudhanshu got unconcius.{if you can't understand plz read take a look at the first two lines}.Hari tried many to make Sudhanshu concius,but he failed.Hari was just joking, he just said that " from many days i am experiencing many unusual things so today i went to meet a tantrik" and the tantrik told that there is a negative energy in the surrounding of your house.Sudhanshu came back in concius mind after one hour.Hari was gone to a shop to buy daily needs.Sudhanshu was very scared when he saw that there is no Hari.He was shouting Hari Hari are you here,meanwhile Hari came in and said ohh! thank god you came back in concius mind. Sudhanshu was scared.

Many days passed. One day Hari had some urgent work in the village so wished to take Sudhanshu with him, but Sudhanshu did not want to take leave from his job.So after two days Hari decided to go alone and he told Sudhanshu that he will come in 7 days. After that Sudhanshu was very scared and did not move out of the house after coming from Mishra sweethouse. Three days passed.
In the night of third day it was raining and sounds of thunderstoms were troubling Sudhanshu.He can't sleep till 1AM because of fear. Hari in the village was busy doing his work but unfortunately he forgot an important paper to bring that he asked his cousin who was in Indore so the cousin went to
Hari's house so when he was just turning to the way of Hari's house Sudhanshu got alert mode he thought may be a theif is coming or may be Hari so he moved to the door of the house with stick in one hand, meanwhile the cousin's bike slipped as it was raining so the land was paddy at that time and the cousin fell down in the wet land and the bike was moving far from his reach,and when Sudhanshu

opended the door he did not saw any bike or any person so he thought it was just an illusion,

so he was just going to close the door when the cousin called him excuse me.Sudhanshu got scared and he can't dare look back but after making himself prepared he turned back but as the cousin fell from the bike so he was injured and struck in mud, he can't stand. When Sudhanshu saw no one he was very scared but the cousin again said excuse me who is there?Sudhanshu shouted who is there?The cousin replied it's me cousin of Hari but Sudhanshu could not hear him as there was lightning at that time.so he can't hear but he saw someone in the mud so he shouted in fear "don't come near me,hey mighty soul plz leave me " meanwhile the cousin recognized Sudhanshu as they were from same village and he knows that Sudhanshu is the only guy who is scared from ghosts this much.

So to tell Sudhanshu who is he, the cousin tried to stand and go near him, but as he tried to stand Sudhanshu started to yell " No don't come here plz leave me" and Sudhanshu fell from the stairs and the cOusin ran near Sudhanshu and as he started runing Sudhanshu fainted. Then the cousin took him in the house and waited for him to be normal. After 1 hour he came back and when he saw a man sitting infront of him in his house he shouted and slapped the cousin and start kicking, punching the cousin, when the cousin shouted "bro it's me Vinayak" then Sudhanshu felt relieved.

Then asked Vinayak what are you doing here? Vinayak replied bro i am here to take the documents that hari has told me to take from your house. Ohh! exclaimed Sudhanshu then he gave him the documents and said to wait for the morning. In the morning Sudhanshu took leave from his job and made a plan to visit the village with

Vinayak. So he reached the village and came back with Hari.. ————————END------------

CHAPTER TWENTY-SEVEN

THE MYSTERIOUS TEDDY

Sandie Slaughterhouse was just like any ordinary sixteen year old girl who was living in beesting, a town in honeycomb, Beesting, a very beautiful hill station. She was 16 years old and was living with her uncle and aunt. She was an introvert girl, was into parties. She liked to be alone, even at home she used to be in her room alone, doing her homeorks and rest of time she used to sit near the window and look in the sky. Crying in the night, smiling in the morning this was her routine. She was there but her heart her mind was somewhere else. She was a very kind girl, never replied to anyone's troll or comment, just smile and move.

As usual, one night she was sitting on a chair near the window, looking in the sky and was making a sketch. She heard some noice, she got up and looked through the window. What is that! she shouted in a stressful voice, Oh my god! is that a teddy? she questioned. A small teddy walked up through the pipe and stood on the surface of the window and knocked on the window. Sandie was sweating, she fell on her bed in shock, her eyes wide open. She was not able to believe what she saw. Teddy knocked again, he was trying to open the window. Sandie stood up immediately and grabbed a stick and hit the teddy with that. The teddy fell shouting on the road in a mud. "Eww" expressed his emotions. The teddy was stuck in the mud, he was facing a lot of problems in getting up. He found a stick beside him, pick that small stick and was trying to release himself from the mud with the help of mud. He gave many attempts but failed and unfortunately the stick broke. The teddy was teriffied, was confused what to do. A middle-aged man was passing by that road, he was partially drunk, he saw that teddy, he stood there for about 5 minutes then picked up the teddy and took to his home. Teddy reached his home, the man gave that teddy to his daughter. The man's whole family sat on the dinning table and the girl kept the teddy in her room.

"I have to get out of here at any cost" said teddy. He opened the door slightly and moved out. He saw the main door and thought to get out. As soon as he ran towards the door, the girl saw the teddy and shouted "is the teddy running himself dad!" and walked towards the teddy. The teddy lyed on the floor to avoid the situation. The girl picked the teddy and walked back to dad. She expressed that "hey, dad! i myself put the teddy in the room, but it was lying there near the main door" Her dad did not paid attention, and all he said was "no dear, maybe you forgot to put it in the room" Now the girl went into her room with the teddy and put the teddy on table and crawled up her bed. It was very tough for the teddy to get out, he now decided to get down from the table and try to escape from the window. He was getting down from the table very carefully so that no one could have an idea. After coming down, he was having another problem that was to open and escape through the window. He wasn successful in opening the window but as soon as he stepped outside the window, his other leg pushed a showpiece and it produced a sound when it fell. The teddy jumped hurriedly thinking that the sound will awake the girl.

CHAPTER TWENTY-EIGHT

TACTLESS SPIRIT

Intelligent psychiatrist MR STEVEN PARKES is arguing with patient teacher MISS DORIS CONNOR. STEVEN tries to hug DORIS but she shakes him off.

STEVEN:
Please Doris, don't leave me.
DORIS:
I'm sorry Steven, but I'm looking for somebody a bit more brave. Somebody who faces his fears head on, instead of running away.
STEVEN:
I am such a person!
DORIS frowns.

DORIS:
I'm sorry, Steven. I just don't feel excited by this relationship anymore.
DORIS leaves.

STEVEN sits down, looking defeated.

Moments later, admirable author LADY MORWENNA SNOZCUMBER barges in looking flustered.

STEVEN:
Goodness, Morwenna! Is everything okay?
MORWENNA:

I'm afraid not.

STEVEN:

What is it? Don't keep me in suspense...

MORWENNA:

It's ... a Spirit ... I saw an evil Spirit frame a bunch of baby birds!

STEVEN:

Defenseless baby birds?

MORWENNA:

Yes, defenseless baby birds!

STEVEN:

Bloomin' heck, Morwenna! We've got to do something.

MORWENNA:

I agree, but I wouldn't know where to start.

STEVEN:

You can start by telling me where this happened.

MORWENNA:

I was...

MORWENNA fans herself and begins to wheeze.

   STEVEN:

Focus Morwenna, focus! Where did it happen?

MORWENNA:

Vasquez Rocks, California! That's right - Vasquez Rocks, California!

STEVEN springs up and begins to run.

EXT. A ROAD - CONTINUOUS

   STEVEN rushes along the street, followed by MORWENNA. They take a short cut through some back gardens, jumping fences along the way.

EXT. VASQUEZ ROCKS, CALIFORNIA - SHORTLY AFTER

MOLLY RUSSELL a tactless Spirit terrorises two baby birds.

STEVEN, closely followed by MORWENNA, rushes towards MOLLY, but suddenly stops in his tracks.

MORWENNA:

What is is? What's the matter?

STEVEN:

That's not just any old Spirit, that's Molly Russell!

MORWENNA:

Who's Molly Russell?

STEVEN:

Who's Molly Russell? Who's Molly Russell? Only the most tactless Spirit in the universe!

MORWENNA:

Blinkin' knickers, Steven! We're going to need some help if we're going to stop the most tactless Spirit in the universe!

STEVEN:

You can say that again.

MORWENNA:

Blinkin' knickers, Steven! We're going to need some help if we're going to stop the most tactless Spirit in the universe!

STEVEN:

I'm going to need stone, lots of stone.

Molly turns and sees Steven and Morwenna. She grins an evil grin.

MOLLY:

Steven Parkes, we meet again.

MORWENNA

You've met?

STEVEN:

Yes. It was a long, long time ago...

EXT. A PARK - BACK IN TIME

A young STEVEN is sitting in a park listening to some orchestral music, when suddenly a dark shadow casts over him.

He looks up and sees MOLLY. He takes off his headphones.

MOLLY:

Would you like some peppermints?

STEVEN's eyes light up, but then he studies MOLLY more closely, and looks uneasy.

STEVEN:

I don't know, you look kind of tactless.

MOLLY:

Me? No. I'm not tactless. I'm the least tactless Spirit in the world.

STEVEN:

Wait, you're a Spirit?

STEVEN runs away, screaming.

EXT. VASQUEZ ROCKS, CALIFORNIA - PRESENT DAY
  MOLLY

You were a coward then, and you are a coward now.

MORWENNA:

(To STEVEN) You ran away?

STEVEN:

(To MORWENNA) I was a young child. What was I supposed to do?

STEVEN turns to MOLLY.

STEVEN:

I may have run away from you then, but I won't run away this time!

STEVEN runs away.

He turns back and shouts.

STEVEN:

I mean, I am running away, but I'll be back - with stone.

MOLLY:

I'm not scared of you.

STEVEN:

You should be.

EXT. A GREASY DINER - LATER THAT DAY

STEVEN and MORWENNA walk around searching for something.

STEVEN:

I feel sure I left my stone somewhere around here.

MORWENNA:

Are you sure? It does seem like an odd place to keep deadly stone.

STEVEN:

You know nothing Morwenna Snozcumber.

MORWENNA:

We've been searching for ages. I really don't think they're here.

Suddenly, MOLLY appears, holding a pair of stone.

MOLLY:

Looking for something?

MORWENNA:

Crikey, Steven, she's got your stone.

STEVEN:

Tell me something I don't already know!

MORWENNA:

The earth's circumference at the equator is about 40,075 km.

STEVEN:

I know that already!

MORWENNA:

.

MOLLY:

(appalled) Dude!

While MOLLY is looking at MORWENNA with disgust, STEVEN lunges forward and grabs his deadly stone. He wields them, triumphantly.

STEVEN:

Prepare to die, you tactless sprout!

MOLLY:

No please! All I did was frame a bunch of baby birds!

DORIS enters, unseen by any of the others.

STEVEN:

I cannot tolerate that kind of behaviour! Those baby birds were defenceless! Well now they have a defender - and that's me! Steven Parkes defender of innocent baby birds.

MOLLY

Don't hurt me! Please!

STEVEN:

Give me one good reason why I shouldn't use these stone on you right away!

MOLLY:

Because Steven, I am your mother.

STEVEN looks stunned for a few moments, but then collects himself.

STEVEN:

No you're not!

MOLLY:

Ah well, it had to be worth a try.

MOLLY tries to grab the stone but STEVEN dodges out of the way.

STEVEN:

Who's the mummy now? Huh? Huh?

Unexpectedly, MOLLY slumps to the ground.

MORWENNA:
Did she just faint?
STEVEN:
I think so. Well that's disappointing. I was rather hoping for
a more dramatic conclusion, involving my deadly stone.
STEVEN crouches over MOLLY's body.
MORWENNA:
Be careful, Steven. It could be a trick.
STEVEN:
No, it's not a trick. It appears that... It would seem... Molly
Russell is dead!
STEVEN:
What?
STEVEN:
Yes, it appears that I scared her to death.
MORWENNA claps her hands.
MORWENNA:
So your stone did save the day, after all.
DORIS steps forward.
DORIS:
Is it true? Did you kill the tactless Spirit?
STEVEN:
Doris how long have you been...?
DORIS puts her arm around STEVEN.
DORIS:
Long enough.
STEVEN:
Then you saw it for yourself. I killed Molly Russell.
DORIS:
Then the baby birds are safe?
STEVEN:
It does seem that way!
A crowd of vulnerable baby birds enter, looking relived.

DORIS:

You are their hero.

The baby birds bow to STEVEN.

STEVEN:

There is no need to bow to me. I seek no worship. The knowledge that Molly Russell will never frame baby birds ever again, is enough for me.

DORIS:

You are humble as well as brave!

One of the baby birds passes STEVEN a magic stone

DORIS:

I think they want you to have it, as a symbol of their gratitude.

STEVEN:

I couldn't possibly.

Pause.

STEVEN:

Well, if you insist.

STEVEN takes the stone.

STEVEN:

Thank you.

The baby birds bow their heads once more, and leave.

STEVEN turns to DORIS.

STEVEN:

Does this mean you want me back?

DORIS:

Oh, Steven, of course I want you back!

STEVEN smiles for a few seconds, but then looks defiant.

STEVEN:

Well you can't have me.

DORIS:

WHAT?

STEVEN:

You had no faith in me. You had to see my scare a Spirit to death before you would believe in me. I don't want a lover like that.
DORIS:
But...
STEVEN:
Please leave. I want to spend time with the one person who stayed with me through thick and thin - my best friend, Morwenna.
MORWENNA grins.
DORIS:
But...
MORWENNA:
You heard the gentleman. Now be off with you. Skidaddle! Shoo!
DORIS:
Steven?
STEVEN:
I'm sorry Doris, but I think you should skidaddle.
DORIS leaves.
MORWENNA turns to STEVEN.
MORWENNA:
Did you mean that? You know ... that I'm your best friend?
STEVEN:
Of course you are!
The two walk off arm in arm.
Suddenly MORWENNA stops.
MORWENNA:
When I said , you know I was just trying to distract the Spirit don't you?
THE END